A·LION·FOR·LEWIS

New York   The Dial Press

A·LION·FOR·LEWIS

ROSEMARY WELLS

TO OMA

Published by
The Dial Press
1 Dag Hammarskjold Plaza
New York, New York 10017

First printing
Design by Atha Tehon

Library of Congress Cataloging in Publication Data
Wells, Rosemary.
A lion for Lewis.
Summary: When Lewis plays make-believe with his
older siblings, he always gets the least desirable role until
a lion suit found in a corner turns him into a king.
[1. Brothers and sisters—Fiction.
2. Play—Fiction] I. Title.
PZ7.W46843Li   [E]   82-70197   AACR2
ISBN 0-8037-4683-0
ISBN 0-8037-4686-5 (lib. bdg.)

The art consists of watercolor paintings that are
camera-separated and reproduced in full color.

"I'll be the mother," said Sophie.
"And I'll be the father," said George.

"What can I be?" asked Lewis.

"You can be the baby," said George.

"All right," said Lewis.

Lewis was fed and changed and put to bed.

"Now can I be the father?" asked Lewis. "Or the mother?"

"That's over," said Sophie. "I'm a doctor now."

"And I'm the head nurse," said George.

"But what about me? What shall I be?" asked Lewis.

"You can be sick, then," said Sophie.

"All right," said Lewis.

George gave Lewis ten shots.

Sophie bandaged him up.

Then they gave him some medicine and put him to bed.

"Now can I be the doctor?" asked Lewis. "Or the nurse?"

"That's over," said Sophie. "I'm a princess now."

"And I'm a prince," said George.

"Can I be something?" asked Lewis.

"Stay down there, Lewis, and hold this tight," said George.

"All right," said Lewis.

Lewis held it for a long, long time.

Then he shouted, "I'm coming back now."

"I want to be the king," said Lewis.

"We need a maid," said Sophie.

"You can be the maid," said George.

"NO!" said Lewis.

Lewis went far, far away,
to the darkest corner of the attic and watched the rain.
Watching Lewis was a lion.
It didn't move.

"Maybe it's dead," said Lewis.
He tickled it.

It was only a lion suit.
Lewis put it on

and zipped it up.

Then Lewis shouted,
"Help! I've been eaten by a lion!"
"Silly," said George.
"Nonsense," said Sophie.

Lewis stepped forward.
"Help!" shrieked Sophie.
"Don't eat us!" yelled George.

Lewis in the lion crept closer and closer.

"Are you in there, Lewis?" yelled George.
"Can you hear us, Lewis?" yelled Sophie.
 Inside Lewis growled.

"Stop him, Lewis!" said Sophie.
"Bite him from the inside, Lewis!" said George.

"I'll try!" squeaked Lewis.

So Lewis swatted and kicked,
and the lion roared.

And Lewis pummeled and pounded
and thumped and bumped inside the lion...

until the lion gave up and Lewis popped out,
shouting, "I'm the king!"

"Oh, Lewis!" said Sophie and George.
"Where did that lion come from?"

"He's mine," said Lewis.

Easy Books

7261

Easy Books   7261

E
W   Wells, Rosemary
          A lion for Lewis

DATE		
NOV 26 1986		
1-31 DEC 17 2001		
FEB 1988		
MAY 07 1991		

JAN 12 1988

JAN 26 1988

FEB 9   1988